I0745008

SHUFFLE

an anthology of microlit

edited by

Cassandra Atherton

SPINELESS WONDERS
www.shortaustralianstories.com.au

Spineless Wonders
PO Box 220
STRAWBERRY HILLS
New South Wales, Australia, 2012
shortaustralianstories.com.au

First published by Spineless Wonders 2019
Text copyright © remains with individual authors.
Cover image and design by Richard Holt

Editorial assistance by Jennifer Leung, Kalhari Jayaweera, Hannah Janssen and Hannah Oakshott.
Layout by Bronwyn Mehan.

All rights reserved. Without limiting the rights under copyright reserved above, no part of this publication may be produced, stored in or introduced into a retrieval sysem, or transmitted, in any form or by any means (electronic, mechanical, photocopying, recording or otherwise) without the prior written permission of the publisher of this book.

Typeset in Franklin Gothic Book
Printed and bound by Ingram Spark
ISBN 978-1-925052-43-5

Shuffle, an anthology of microlit/
Atherton, Cassandra (ed)

Distribution in Australia and New Zealand by New South

Aboriginal and Torres Strait Islander readers are advised that this book contains the name of a person who has died.

A catalogue record for this book is available from the National Library of Australia

Matrimony is baloney
She'll be wanting alimony
In a year or so
Still they go and shuffle
Shuffle Off to Buffalo
When she knows as much as we know
She'll be on her way to Reno
While he still has dough
She'll give him the Shuffle
When they're back from Buffalo

AL DUBIN

Contents

Introduction

Still they go and shuffle

When I heard the title of this year's anthology was going to be *Shuffle*, I was immediately taken back to my late teens when I played the part of Peggy Sawyer in an amateur production of *42nd Street*. 'Shuffle off to Buffalo', the name of a basic tap step, was transformed into a song and tap dance extravaganza, replete with sequins and marcel waves in this musical. I remember thinking that one day I'd like to go to Buffalo, if everyone was shuffling off there! While this might seem tangential, tap dancing is all about syncopation, splitting beats and making music. And this is what the writers in this anthology all have in common; they are all working with sound in sophisticated ways.

Recognising the popularity and complexity of microlit, Spineless Wonders continues to extend its publishing into exciting multi-platform collaborations. In keeping with this theme, a selection of texts from this anthology will form the basis of a series of commissioned works by Sonant Bodies, an experimental sound-art collective.

The promotion for the Newcastle Writers Festival/joanne burns Microlit Award features an iPod Shuffle – those petite devices that initially weighed 22 grams and stored up to 240 songs – and while it's now discontinued, it is still a brilliant metaphor for microlit. Indeed, the second and fourth generations of iPod Shuffles were square and perhaps akin to a paragraph of microlit. In this way, both the iPod and the microlit are subversive in the way their extensive content belies their small exteriors. Indeed, a bit like the 'Shuffle off to Buffalo' epigraph, they can look benign but when you start reading they can be highly charged and quite political narratives.

Very short literary forms are proliferating online and in print. While traditional literary genres, such as the novel, short story, lineated lyric poetry and drama have been at the centre of literary practice for centuries, contemporary writers are reinvigorating our understanding of genre with new and sometimes unique approaches to form. Spineless Wonders employs the term 'microlit' to encompass all short forms – including prose poetry and microfiction. The differences between short fiction forms, such as flash fiction and sudden prose, are often debated in scholarship, with debates generally centring on the length of works. However, it is the distinction between the relatively broad categories of microfiction and prose poetry that most often troubles writers and critics. What constitutes the greatest distinction between the two is that prose poetry is a form of poetry and microfiction and its counterparts are forms of prose narrative. This is important, because it emphasises that short prose forms may be poetical or prosaic, and offers a way of understanding key divergences between different kinds of works.

Many readers of very short forms enjoy all varieties, and therefore, they are not necessarily interested in the finer points of nomenclature or genre. In the same way, this anthology avoids labelling each piece of microlit, ultimately letting the reader decide whether they are reading microfiction, prose poetry or other examples of the short form. *Shuffle* is more interested in rhapsodising the short form, than in breaking it into its different varieties. Similarly, instead of placing all the microfiction together and all of the prose poetry together, or all the humorous pieces in one section and pieces about nature in another, the order of microlit in this collection is intended to be more like the experience of listening to songs on shuffle mode – you never quite know what is coming next!

Shuffle celebrates the theme of sound: from the streets of Rome at night; the personification of ice cubes; David Bowie; Mad Max; a chainsaw; fish flops and tiny pikelets, to a conversation through a thin wall and silence. The microlit references sound in a plethora of unexpected ways; putting the short form under a kind of glorious pressure to showcase each writer's unique abstractions.

Congratulations to those shortlisted for the Newcastle Writers Festival/joanne burns Microlit Award and to all of the writers who entered the competition. This year the standard of microlit was so high that we had to create a longlist, a shortlist and a short-shortlist (quite appropriate for an anthology on the short form). It was writing that attempted to explore sound in unexpected ways that was the most successful of the microlit pieces. The two winning pieces are, for the National category, 'Birding' by Brenda Saunders and for the Hunter category, 'Fish Flops and Flops ' by Jan Dean. These pieces of microlit are remarkable for their impressive control and use of memorable imagery.

Thank you to Sonant Bodies composers, Victoria Pham, James

Hazel, Kezia Yap, Sarah Monk and Stephen Adams.

Thank you to Rosemarie Milsom, director of the Newcastle Writers Festival and her team for her foresight in sponsoring this award and her phenomenal work in bringing it to the fabulous Newcastle Writers Festival – one of the finest and most supportive writers' festivals in Australia.

Thank you to the commissioned writers: Jordie Albiston, Shady Cosgrove, Jen Craig, Shastra Deo, Richard Holt, Jill Jones, Bella Li, David McCooey, Geoff Page, Hazel Smith and Anna Spargo-Ryan, whose pieces of microlit are brilliantly conceived and wonderfully textured in their showcasing of the glistering possibilities for the short form.

Thank you to Richard Holt for his alluring cover design and his poignant piece of microlit in this anthology. Thank you to joanne burns, after whom this award is named. joanne is a pioneer and ambassador of the short form and her luminous, witty and innovative microlit is enduring.

Finally, thank you to Spineless Wonders' publisher, Bronwyn Mehan, for her devotion to the short form. We appreciate her tireless efforts to provide writers with exciting ways to showcase their work both on the page and in the most amazing ways off the page.

Cassandra Atherton, 2019

Jill Jones

ALL THAT SHUDDER

That year, I went back to the city alone, me and all my noisy solitude. I remember the way we'd gossip stories into night, along those roads, Glebe Point Road, Darlinghurst Road. Or walk to the harbour, listen to the wharves, what's left of them. Or get wasted in a loud pub to the south, towards Botany, where the planes almost drown.

Or I'm back at that corner where she said I should accept things as they are, rather than holding out something to be filled. But the glass has passed. I hear it smash to the gutter.

I remember helping another girl throw up, just here, in another century after a night nearby with booming walls, of all that survival in tune with a kiss, names and numbers on drink coasters, promises as opposed to meanings, too many women not watching you. So there I was, being gentle with this kid retching, as hellhounds scoured her insides. Night allows this tact and touch. Then she walked off. They always do.

I'm here again, listening as night's sirens shift away. Like a reprieve, like an unprepared morning. There's nothing butch in the sound of dawn, lost harmonies, or sleep.

David McCooey

GESANG DER JÜNGLINGE (SONG OF THE YOUTHS)

Every Christmas, my mother would play war-time Bing Crosby. My father would counter with the Choir of King's College, Cambridge. The boy choristers were school children, like me. But my class only sang carols each summer at the old people's home down the road. Most of our audience looked like they had given up eating. We sung 'Silent Night' as we were taught to, without slurring on 'peace'. At ten, I discovered 'Happy Xmas (War is Over)', but that was before school choirs sang John Lennon.

In high school – Christmas carols behind me – I bought so many records that I would sneak them into my bedroom. One day, I arrived home with Karlheinz Stockhausen's *Gesang der Jünglinge*, with its mix of electronic sound and a recording of a boy soprano shuffled around the stereo field. Stockhausen had planned to write a mass, but he was told that loudspeakers had no place in a church. On this day, my father caught me before I could reach my bedroom, and he asked to see what I had bought. I sheepishly slipped the record out of its paper bag and showed him. 'I don't give you pocket money to buy Stockhausen,' he said. 'But it's Deutsche Grammophon,' I said, pointing to the august yellow label, and he laughed.

Years later, I told this story at my father's funeral service. As I spoke, I could hear the sound of my father's old friends shuffling their feet on the chapel floor, and my young son – untouched by the fires of memory – calling out that he was hungry.

Bella Li

THE ROCK

Somewhere between the laundry aisle and the junk food section, my favourite track from my favourite album by my favourite '90s post-rock outfit starts playing over the PA, and it's a banger, it's the best twelve and a half minutes of my life. Suddenly I have six boxes of Cadbury Favourites in the trolley and I don't know how they got there. I'm about to reach down and put two of them back on the shelf and then the droning guitar in the extended seven-minute bridge gets louder and I think, what the hell, why not, you only live once, don't stop believing! All the other shoppers are coasting along, perched on their trolleys, with jars of pickles and Best Foods mayonnaise crammed inside, really both living *and* believing. By the time I get to the end and see the fruits and vegetables piled into slippery, gleaming stacks like Tahoe in summer, I'm ready to marry anyone, I'm ready to sign away the rights to all the unwritten film scripts I haven't written. There's a man to my right gracefully peeling three bananas from a bunch of five. Right before the key change I think it might be Dwayne (The Rock), but it's not.

Anna Spargo-Ryan

MENIERE'S

When I am eight I open my lungs in a school music room and I do not close them again. I do trills and scales and *Lean on Me* at school speech night and *Quando m'en vo* beside a grand piano and Puccini in a concert hall. I break my neck with an E6 and shake hands with Michael Crawford and am invited to a masterclass on banks of the Tiber. I am addicted to the sounds my body makes: the heartbeat of vibrato, the great gold waves of my spirit being tuned, the applause.

And then I am thirty.

On a cold morning everything is muffled.

I can't get enough sound in. I start to say pardon? like an old lady.

I feel like I'm inside a bucket.

I feel like I need to open a window.

I tell the doctor: *Help. I think something's stuck in my ears.*

He has a lamp on a stick. He uses it to look for the music.

Instead he finds the ends of my vestibular nerves. He says ah.

The damage is permanent. It is degenerative.

It is a suffocation. I choke on my impenetrable plasticine ears.

The stillness is deafening.

Andy Kissane

DRIVING WITH GURRUMUL

I let the glorious voice of Gurrumul wash over me as I drive. I wonder what Gurrumul, who was born blind, made of photographs. They would have barely existed for him, although he would have been photographed for album covers and by his family and friends. Photographs endure, they record a moment in time, but music transcends time. I love turning my car into a mini auditorium filled with sound, a dark room where I grip the steering wheel and travel into the bones of the melody, its sinews seeping into me the way an image suddenly emerges from the emulsion tray. I love the intense privacy of the car and how it gives me the opportunity to drift, dwell and reside in music. Sometimes the wow moment of my day happens when I am stuck on some freeway that has morphed into a carpark, my eyes closed, the music blasting out of the speakers and bathing me in colour, in a world soaking with percussive pleasures, astonishing riffs, fingers that can coax such beauty from a twelve string guitar, a voice that cuts like headlights through the night. Is this what life was like for Gurrumul, all the time?

Geoff Page

LESTER AT THE END

Lester Young 1909–1959

And then that big room at the Alvin, looking down on Birdland
where the younger players came and went, acknowledging a debt.
And nowhere near forgotten yet are still those fifteen months'
humiliation, courtesy the US Army being brave elsewhere. His
thoughts perhaps are linear; his solos 'always told a story', the
chords more felt than heard. The sound that once was 'airy' is
harder these days to obtain although a sort of discipline his
father had instilled in him survives beneath the pain, the ache
of ruined teeth, the burned oesophagus, the liver almost done.

Just now there's been a stint in Paris, abandoned by agreement;
a late discovery of absinthe topping up the gin. And, on the plane,
a handkerchief flowering with his blood. On the bed there at the
Alvin they say his lips and fingers, deprived now of an instrument,
spelt out a final phrase.

Mark O'Flynn

THIN WALL

Listening through the wall I hear a man talking on speaker phone to his dying mother. They speak of the weather and comfortable pillows and hospital meals. He tells her he will be coming to see her soon, as soon as his day release is organised and sponsors approved. Many forms to fill. They will hold hands and talk over old times and everything that is going to be all right. He will tell her of his plans. There is silence. The silence of loss that has yet to arrive. He tells her that his time is up. Only six minutes allowed. The sound of her voice saying goodbye is too much. There is a moment through the thin wall I do not want to hear. He hangs up and goes back to his work of sweeping the path, the hoarse scratching bristles of the broom the sound of grief wheezing its worst, a path which has been swept and swept a thousand times already.

Emma Ashmere

CALENTURE

She was always handy with a pitchfork, not for the grapes, but for the growers when they came too close. Trucks trembled the weighbridge. Water dripped from tailgates, a trick to bump up the weight. We were swarmed by bees and watched by the men as we tested the sugar, the pH. We took turns with the forklift, from the truck to the crusher to the truck from the crusher, grapes, leaves, sticks, spiders, snakes.

On night shift we rigged up the heat exchanger and a pump and filled the shallow concrete tank. After midnight-lunch we lay on our backs, steam rising to the stars. On my last day, I leapt up behind her up the clanging steps up the highest vat, tall as a mast. We opened the lid in that particular way so we wouldn't fall in.

She asked if I'd be coming back for next year's vintage. I'd already booked my ticket back, and looked down at the valley now fenced, cleared, striped with vines, and saw the old mass and tangle of eucalypts and thought of those sailors who'd been too long at sea and mistook the grey waves for the green fields of home.

Hilary Hewitt

LEARNING A LANGUAGE

My friend Maryam knows everything about everything. She says felines don't talk in the wild; miaow is a language derived from human contact. I try some basic vocab on the skinny black male who suns himself on my back roof, a few tongue rolls and chirps. He stares as though I'm speaking a foreign language. Big yellow eyes. *Would you like a bowl of milk? Seafood casserole? Yes, that's a worm tablet. Can I have a pat?* His reply? A yawning hiss. Should I invite him inside? Maryam says I'm addicted to bad boys, but what would she know.

When Black Cat falls from the roof, he glares as though it's my fault and drags himself into the shrubbery. What if he dies? Maryam says felines fall on their feet; I buy more seafood casserole, just in case. Next morning Blackie is back on the roof, washing his paws. *Clink clink* says the spoon in the KitEkat tin. He draws himself into sphinx position. When he hisses he reminds me of Dad, but now I understand. We're all scared. Then, a tiny *miaow*. I can't wait to tell Maryam.

Jordie Albiston

DISCONCERT

once we escape to Echuca   endeavour to discard the
discordant days for a while   there are trees trees & the
birds of winged trees flying our names high above   what
is it that we don't hear?   I open up my discontent chest
pull out the dysmorphic part   place it on an altar of
earth & depart   yes walking helps & here is the water
the Wakiti Creek   & corellas & cockies & crows & galahs
they orchestrate it my rapture   & when I return there
are eucalypts humming beneath my skin   & the birds
& the birds of all the winged trees sing out from within
laarv! laarv!   & I am a cymbal a song on a stage with
you vanishing vanishing like vibrating air from a gong for
an age   a disaggregation   a disconcert of loss   & I sit
here loving I sit here loving & disappear into a dysphasic
key where I am alone & all of it stops & everything falls
like feathers & see God is gone

Julie Chevalier

A LITTLE GYM MUSIC

after 'Send in the Clowns' from *A Little Night Music*

women aging disgracefully   balancing on forearms and toes
straight as a proverbial   opposite knee to opposite elbow   no
harbour bridges   still waiting   we almost levitate   you? in
mid-air   me? ready to leap   bliss this late?   more like the
torture of indecision   start losing my timing   knowing *the door
to your room was   the door to mine*[1]   the humiliation of hiding
you don't want what i want?   *mea culpa*, my dear   dry white
fingertips losing their grip   who wants a scrawny old   late in
the routine for abs cycle   should be up to stretches   stretches
for flappy arms   the hammies: cloud-clowns of the muscular
world   the bi- tri- quadricep clouds, the lats clouds, cat stretch
clouds & a few yoga clouds   a clown endorphin high   replace
the equipment   skin dry as saint joan's wishbone   send in
kids the size of fit balls   kidding myself   you'll never leave   a
moment for the aloe vera tissues   a latte & a raspberry almond
friand before the convent minibus   you bloody well could if you
wanted to

1. Words in italics by Anne Sexton

Sandra Renew

LESBIAN CONTENT

I am employed as *Lesbian Content*[1] to tick boxes demonstrating gender and sexuality friendliness. The tick is a small self-satisfied noise in HR Recruitment. *Job Done!*

This job is a silent one. No ostentatious, obvious raising of LGBTIQAAA+ issues, themes or words to complicate the normal routines and outputs. Just a brooding accusatory, no noise presence – *I'm watching you, and listening in.*

I silently lesbian in coffee machine clusters, water cooler leaning, and staff meeting tables. Silently lesbianing at a hot desk in open plan Department of Everything. Lesbianing without comment at staff barbeques and *Fun Run Government is of the people* days.

In the end, you are lesbian-ed without ever knowing. You may, one day, suddenly realise that your mind is not quite as made up as it once was. Or that your knee-jerk reaction to the alphabetising LGBTIQAAA is one of shouting what the letters stand for, rather than jumping into bashing a poofter. The change is all yours. You have been lesbianed. My job is done.

1. The term 'lesbian content' was used by Hannah Gadsby in her stand-up comedy show *Nanette*, Netflix Original 2018. Directors Jan Olb & Madeleine Parry. However, the concept has been explored in a textual discourse analysis by Hélène Cixous, used in my PhD thesis *Acting Like a Girl* (University of New England, 1994).

Cynthia Troup

SUSPENSION (DESTRUCTION)

A chorus, of sorts. Percussive. Swirling. As dense as rapt applause in a chamber music hall. Then sparse, as if strokes of a skipping rope were stirring the air and the ground, air and ground, air … ground … air …

A near-freezing dawn, early in the coldest month. Beyond thin bursts of city traffic you're listening now, to concerted flurries of chirps, unpitched, surrounded by – electrostatic hum? You quicken your stride, which seems excessively loud.

Air ground air ground air … you're a wide-eared tourist, and young. At 260 grams (running on AA batteries), your Sony Walkman Stereo Cassette-Corder seesaws in your pocket. The tiny mic looks like two black dice flung together in your palm.

Just before you round the corner: an intuition of a crowd, hustling, wordless, intent. And elation. Yes yes, a chorus.

Not of feathered birds.

The thaw isn't underfoot, but in international relations. You've stumbled into an ecstasy of destruction and souveniring.

By January 1990, under the gaze of helpless border troops,
more and more 'wall-peckers' – *Mauerspechte* – were demol-
ishing the Berlin Wall by hand, with hammers, chisels, car keys,
pen-knives. This was their clamour at sunrise.

Breathless, you switched your Walkman to 'record'.

Alexandra Geneve

JOHNNY-CAKES

Someone should write about the tiny pikelets that morning and what happened to them. Our mum called them Johnny-Cakes and they were fluffy in the middle with brown, oil-drenched, crunchy edges that bubbled and spat. Topped with raspberry jam (or loquats from the tree outside, remember?) and cream that puddled with the heat, I remember them, for some reason, against the deep blue tiles beneath the window that faced the cliffs.

When the willy-willy came from the north along the coast and moved south-west that morning, away from the water and up onto the land, it brought with it wind, debris, and sharp things that flew. But it took something as well. And not just our Johnny-Cakes. It took people's shadows.

Now we say this is impossible; but we find ourselves thinking *perhaps*. All I know is in that minute-long fury of funnelled wind, we lost more than our home and our carapace against the world. When those windows exploded, outwards mercifully, our shadows were sucked out with the curtains and the old telephone. And that began our very bad year.

Paulette Smythe

WHEN B MOVED IN

When B moved in, the wall became a talking skin. I never saw the man, just heard his meaty grunts and groans as he lugged his stuff upstairs, then the smooth click of a freshly cut key in the lock next door. Late that night the soft creak of another bed a wall away from mine, the slide of warm flesh on cool accommodating sheets, fat ice clinking in a long glass, a moan, a sigh, then music kicking in. Soulful tenor sax blowing close, arcing high to low and back again in the rich milky darkness. B's slow and sultry murmurs ebbed and flowed, a strange tongue millimetres from my ear, chuckling low and coaxing. For thirty nights I prayed I wouldn't sleep, stroked the painted plasterboard, cooed and purred and gasped as lovers do, swore I saw our breath mingling like whispers in the deep wall cavity. Then B moved out. Never saw the man, just caught the thud of something hefty thumping down the stairs and a woman's laughter spilling out in cadent waves.

Shady Cosgrove

AFTERMATH

I'm jerked awake. Metallica. It's shaking the caravan it's so fucking loud. Oh, Jimmy. He's three doors down. Old Sam and Eileen are going to have a fit, you know they are, but he can't help himself. 3 am, and we're all awake now, bearing witness to the memory of a kid just out of high school, fresh in his fatigues. Rage Against the Machine, and I push out of bed, get myself a cuppa. Sit on the front step. Air's so dry it cracks. I can't see the moon but it's there. Shrubs are just outlines. No garbage, though – the desert darkness hides that and this place almost becomes beautiful. Led Zeppelin. He'll be here soon. And sure enough he is. Skinny. Eyes ringed red. Same shirt he's been wearing for three days. 'Come here, Jimmy.' And he falls into my arms, sobbing.

Bonny Cassidy

CULTURAL STUDS

Could it ever be plausible, or even ethical, to portray Mad Max as happy?[1]

Ross Gibson asked this before Max reappeared, from the nuke wastes of Sydney, in Namibia. When Max was still an expert, and we believed in these. Is that what Max thinks about as he leaks onto the badlands – the rented flat in Elouera; night surfing, macramé? Back then he was natural, that is, a family of experts.

That was my childhood home; a couple of times we went to see the fuselage jutting from the sands. I couldn't really accept the wreck wasn't history. Driving on, we'd end up at the cairn that marks Cook's landing. According to Stephen Muecke, this monument possesses *contiguous magic*.[2] Like an amulet against the amplification of trauma, maybe.

The dunes have been transported. Who goes there? A billowing cloud.

Max's new unhappiness is penance, not vengeance. He buckles into his burden: chain, muzzle, file and a tattoo of his dead baby's name. Now his family is a field of strangers, which is radically ethical. Mark Davis said this is an illustration of Australian culture *with the fences down,*[3] but if you listen carefully there are microclimates and eyries. There is dankness in the permanent noon. There are experts without jobs.

In the dry lands a teenager teaches herself guitar, bungling the bridge, her notes skittering down, hyphenated.

1. Ross Gibson, *South of the West: Postcolonialism and the Narrative Construction of Australia*, Indiana University Press, 1992 (177).
2.Stephen Muecke, 'A Touching and Contagious Captain Cook: Thinking History through Things', in *History, Power, Text: Cultural Studies and Indigenous Studies*, eds. Timothy Neale, Crystal McKinnon and Eve Vincent, CSR Books, 2014: 153-166 (153).
3.Mark Davis, 'Who Shot the Albatross? Gate-keeping in Australian Culture', University of Adelaide, April 27, 2018.

Shastra Deo

PAVLOVSK STATION

Protoplasm is in perpetual motion. Even with speakers silent the drum of booted feet, bare feet – staccato spilling to shuffle softness – keeps us living. The mother plants still breed true. We're not so different from the fragaria, it seems – both craving milder days, quiet nights. Among rosaceae unrimed it's easy to forget the famine. Siege-song on my tongue to keep from swallowing leaves. Science has yet to prove it, but we know berries grow better with light, water, and the strains of a gardener's tune. Someone will remember this refrain had two parts. Twenty years from now a student of Saint Francis will learn the value of our days. In California fifty years on Phocas reborn will speak of mothers and their daughters, how they dig up the mothers, dig up the daughters, how they'll throw away the mothers and send him the daughters; Fiacre, perhaps, will turn away, and Dorothy will weep. I know no other hymns. There are many saints here. And soon, too, martyrs.

Kathleen Bleakley

POP UP DREAM

i pop home at lunchtime. am surprised to see the neighbours having a party on their front lawn. to hear champagne corks popping. i walk round to my place, hear stilettos clacking on the patio. dolled up women with hats reminding me of prehistoric birds. i ask them what the fuck they're doing here. 1 woman with a particularly hideous hat to match her hideously tight bling bling dress says *it's on your facebook.* as she speaks, i hear her chewing gum and slurping bubbly. *i'm not on facebook. whatever* she says, stuffing popcorn into her red-lipped mouth.

Mark Roberts

GANHABULA

I'm standing at the top of Mount Canobolas/Ganhabula. It is a spring morning, the sun is out, but there is a hint of ice in the breeze which occasionally flicks a piece of yellow tape against the metal framework of a telecommunications tower. This is a return to a place, a connection with country stretching through my family, the hints and suggestions of a buried history, a land that fills the imagination.

I listen to the tape flicking against the metal, like morse code tapping out a message. I listen for a pattern, but the wind swirls around the tower flicking the sound in all directions. Above me I see microwave dishes, mobile cells and other pieces of electronic gadgetry. This is how we communicate. I listen for a hum which would suggest high frequency radio signals are flashing past above my head. But there is nothing but the flicking of the yellow tape.

I become aware of an under layer of sounds. I hear further into the silence – the wind moving through the trees below, the distant sound of a car heading up a dirt road, the faint rumble of a plane invisible in the sky.

Tess Ridgway

IT STRETCHES OUR SHAPE

Part mist at our fingertips, part ambient noise. I'm waving to join you there. I slope down mud banks as bass domes over river rocks. Behind the decks they let off quick spumes of beats and the effect is molten. It's summer & house music rolls my shoulders and leans me back into my heels.

We navigate & boulder downstream amongst the vague shape of others positioned at a depth, goose-fleshed & you exercise a basic differing physical 'right' – to pee freely in the bush. The afternoon whales in in immobile currents; and I wade hip-high after a month-long birth-off of all the *potential* crud from my head but the noise masks the extent of the growth & in the crowd I have to raise my voice till hoarse to be heard. Why do I always want to talk when I'm standing right next to the speakers? 'What are you thinking right now?' 'Which C-grade celeb would you be most freaked out to see here?' But amongst the beer-soaked mud and fug of smoke we see flashes of promise: a near shore low-frequency highest-equivalent that's worth dangling our hands above our head & it stretches our shape– almost billowy.

Brenda Saunders

BIRDING

I have been obsessed with birds for years: going out, recorder in hand, to catch them calling in the wild. But now a scrub wren has found a way to nest inside my head. All day she scratches, flutters her feathers. Pressed tight, her heart beats fast. Magnified it pulses on and on in constant alarm. Her sharp peeps keep me on high alert, drill an ache inside my brain. On and on, she calls the same shrill discordant note. I fear her chicanery. Is she calling for a mate to fill my head, her inner nest with progeny? When will it stop? Will she ever sleep? I have already lost the pace. My inner clock is out of sync, my balance tips in disarray. At night she sits behind my ear, chirps down tunnels, shuffles wings against the drum. I am sure she has grown. Packed in, she blocks all conversation. When I answer I'm misunderstood. I try to explain but the situation is diabolical. Others think I am mad, I see it now. Only in exhausted sleep do I find relief. I dream of escape, digging in dark places. Searching for silence, a kind of peace.

Brenda Proudfoot

DOWN THE RABBIT HOLE

Must you slurp your tea? She'd told him a million times. Nora moved into the other bedroom to escape the sudden snorts and gasps that disturbed her sleep. Stan shuffled along the hallway, bumbled into the bathroom; the slap of the seat against the cistern, the pause and spurt as he peed.

When he forgot how to use the CD player, she celebrated. No more Beethoven, Mahler and Brahms at full volume. He turned on the telly instead. Ads for floor mops and funeral insurance. A football match or a cooking show? How they bickered.

After he collapsed, she visited him in hospital. She looked forward to her lunchtime chat with the girl in the café while she made Nora's flat white. As she ate her home-made sandwiches, she caught snatches of conversation. When Stan slept, she listened for footsteps, the drone of the floor polisher, laughter drifting down the corridor from the nurses' station. She woke when the alarms went off.

After the funeral, there was silence. It was then she began to howl.

Danielle Baldock

SAFE AND SOUND

His calloused hand is warm on hers.

You'll be right, he always says, his voice a deep rumble. Here we are, safe and sound.

They shop together on Tuesdays, when Mum's working and Grandma's volunteering at *Vinnies*. He smells of *Vicks*, and peppermints.

Today, it's rabbits first.

The butchers' shop is cool, meat glowing pink.

How many today, Fred?

Just the one Alf. Just us for tea today.

The portly butcher steps out the back, apron strings cinched tight.

And then she hears the sound. A kind of squelching thump. It ricochets inside her. A wet bright line sprays across the thick sawdust.

The butcher brings out a rustling parcel, neatly folded at the ends.

Now, young lady, something for you.

Smiling, he holds out something limp and pink.

It's a rabbit's foot you see? For luck...

She touches it with unsteady fingers. Her face is hot and red. The fur is soft, toes splayed.

She nods, holds it carefully. The warm foot seems to pulse in time with her blood.

Grandad takes her hand then, closing his fist around fur and flesh and fingers. Takes them home through the bright after-noon, the thump of the butcher's knife echoing behind them.

Richard Holt

DRAGON

After my chores are done I eat the rice balls mother left, then run to where my box is hidden. I take it to the empty pond, place it at the bottom and draw back the lid. ChiChi, the cricket I captured three days ago, scrambles into the shadows. I wait for her to sing.

But there's not a chirp. Without her note to cut the air everything is quiet. The birds have stopped. No breeze stirs the leaves. Then I hear what ChiChi and the birds have heard, an approaching murmur above the clouds. I imagine what kind of monster it must be, its sound so low and menacing that the other creatures honour it with their silence and the world is still for it. I picture what I cannot see as the rumble grows. The beast glides over-head, its outstretched golden wings and flowing beard, its razor talons and smoking nostrils hidden only by the clouds that came over during the morning. And then, as quickly as it has come, the dragon passes, heading in the direction of Nagasaki, where grandmother lives, then on to its far-off lair.

Beth Spencer

BLADE

It was when she tripped over the carpet while walking backwards carrying the chainsaw that things really started to look grim.

Uh oh. Chainsaw? Did I say chainsaw? I meant chain letter. Letter of demand. Eviction notice.

Notice how the light glints on the teeth of the blade.

The carpet was a round black hole, and her foot slipped in.

If she wasn't wearing her diamante buckle slippers she may have been able to save herself, grabbing the edge as she fell.

But the slipper started to slip and she loved those diamonds which reminded her of her mother (who was a bit too rough to love hugely, but, well, you know, enough. You know? hmm. Maybe you do.)

And as she reached one hand down to grasp the slippers she lost her grip, and fell deep deep into that black soft rabbit burrow of depression.

No one knew, and it was months before they came to evict her, and found her. Or found her bones. The letter, the diamante buckled slipper, the abstracted thought, the day that began quite well.

The chainsaw still whirring.

Karen Whitelaw

EARTHQUAKE

When the earthquake struck I was looking in the fridge for something to eat. The fridge shuddered like a dog shaking off water and the light blinked. I jumped back thinking it was about to explode. Behind me the glasses in the cabinet crashed onto the tiles. The air growled.

I thought of Ben surfing, and tsunamis. Desperate, I picked my way barefoot through the broken glass, over the shattered bottle of Veuve his parents gave us for our fifth wedding anniversary, and ran.

The sea was deserted, but hadn't receded.

I raced up the dune to Tess's cottage. She came out onto the porch.

'I was on the beach when the earthquake struck,' she said, her voice breathy. 'I thought an empty coal truck was rumbling down the boat ramp behind me, and the sand shook under its weight. When I looked there was nothing there.'

No, she hadn't seen Ben.

When he came home I was on the front step. I clutched him tightly and he patted my back. He was at the beach, he said, and thought he'd heard an empty coal truck rattling down the boat ramp. But nothing was there.

Hazel Smith

LISTENING

She understood now that she could listen to music in any way she chose. There was no right or wrong way to traverse it, no law about how to open your ears. She could enslave herself to one passage and cut free from the rest, that was her decision. If her attention eloped, she would not be locked up. If she parachuted into the middle of a piece — or sailed with one movement at the expense of another — she did not need to hang her head in shame. She could push the structure to one side or teach it some new tricks. She did not need to be able to articulate the music's inner logic because she could converse with it, and she could allow the sounds to summon any scenario, however bizarre, however remote.

She was not confined by the gurus of musical appreciation, the policemen of musical taste. She was not answerable to the music, nor was the music answerable to her. She could soak in it as it stretched into wider waters and as it sketched its own erratic schedules: migrating without a passport, evading innocence and guilt, posing question after question.

Luke Evans

DA DOOF

I hate nightclubs. They're too loud and the music's invariably shit. What's so good about a DJ anyway? It's just a guy changing the CDs. Every place has one. Now they tour around as if they were famous and people go to see specific ones. What's that all about?

To top it all off, when I'm drunk, the incessant *Doof-doof-doof* noise of the bass makes me literally puke. It fucks me up and I don't know why. I can't stay in the room because my body rejects the music violently.

I like the atmosphere of a pub with a live band. I like to be able to talk to the people I'm out with, which you can't do at a nightclub. No, sir – pubs for me. If I like a band, I become something of a groupie (minus the 'sleeping with the band' part). I'll go exclusively to their gigs, because good house bands are few and far between and I rarely go out. I'm not wasting that time going to some wannabe's concert. This is my Zen time and I have strict criteria that have to be met. I'm not fucking around here, people. This is important.

Moya Costello

RAIN IN THE NORTHERN RIVERS

In the season of thunderstorms, clouds were travelling curiosities, eccentric characters passing through, moving on. Vagabonds, itinerants, swaggies, carnies, troubadours.

Sometimes rain fell like fury, the gods relentless in their punishment of humans.

The morning air was normally blue and bright. But if the forecast was for storms and strong winds, by late afternoon things had stilled in that frightening way at the edge of a precipice overlooking chaos. The air darkened. The wind seized up. Thunder rumbled low. Once-wispy clouds coalesced. There was the thickening cloud with a luminous green underbelly, the blue-green, ultramarine over-colour of Antarctic ice. There was the overhanging cloud, biblical in proportion, with flowery white beard below a dark grey cadence.

The clouds furled and rolled, big surf waves looming low in the pale grey curtain of evening sky. They stalked, until bursting their bellyful of saturating rain.

The rain fell, booming, in heavy banging doors of noise or like long coats or thick, swirling curtains, soaking the air and land, everything dripping, the world become a liquid state. The high treetops were the only visible thing against the skyline, in a drowned landscape.

Sometimes the rain came down like protection, sympathy, shelter.

Jan Dean

FISH FLOPS AND FLAPS

Place your feet into fish flops, the current craze, and your toes peep from plastic mouths. Tails curl behind your heels and an eye bulges over the base of each small toe. They are real to the extreme, almost obscene, either green or gold, but the scaly surface lacks slime. My second toes are longer than the first ones, so would poke out. I spent time in a hospital room with a woman who had similar feet except her second toes were removed because they kept growing longer. Gout had her connected to strong antibiotics. She remained amenable despite intense pain and only cried when placed back in her bed at night. Our malady is called Morton's Toe or Greek Foot, supposedly linked to Greek ancestry, yet although I have motley genealogy including Swedish, Welsh and English, there's no Greek in sight. It is genetic. Long ago my enthusiastic half-sister told me to close my eyes and guess the secret sound while she flip-flopped around the room in her backless slippers of emerald silk, embroidered with colourful flowers; scuffs imported from exotic climes. They were soft relatives of today's mules and slides. The enviable sound, a wondrous *slap, slap,* thrilled.

Susan McCreery

THUNDER-DROP SKY

Her son, on waking: What sound does the sky make?

It depends, she told him, on its mood. Mostly the sky doesn't make a sound.

What mood is it in today?

Looking out the window, she said, Quiet. Reflective.

When he asked what *reflective* meant, she told him the sky was thinking. When he asked her what it was thinking, she said, You can't hear thoughts. Only guess at them.

So the sky doesn't have angry thoughts today?

No, she said. It's unruffled. She explained that *unruffled* meant no messy or torn clouds. Then she told him it was time to get up.

Can you hear what I'm thinking? His face ruffled.

I told you we can't hear thoughts.

I'm an angry sky with dark, torn-up clouds, he said. I am *not* a quiet eflective sky.

R-eflective, she corrected.

And Mum, he said, flipping the covers off. Wanna know what sort of sky you are?

She picked up his shoes and unknotted the laces.

What sort of sky am I?

Thunder-drop sky. But the drops can't get out. The clouds are as big as this house. He widened the distance between his hands. As big as this whole entire universe.

John Carey

LEFT OUT

My left ear has under-stayed its welcome and doesn't do the job it was meant to. Sound is re-crypted into noise. On the phone, I hear voices but the sentences shake out like a cat's-cradle into nonsense. In crowded restaurants the chamber booms like an underwater cavern in a tide-surge. Those who sit on my left are neither seen nor heard and most of my friends are a bit to my Left.

Perversely, machines seem to speak in tongues. My printer says 'coolibah, coolibah', a cunning ploy by the Koreans to boost local sales. A leaf-blower sings 'quit your whinging'.

From the wrong side of the room, Trump on screen must be lip-read ('fabulous' is easy) or interpreted by sign (a hand-gesture like the last flutter of a grounded cheergirl means 'terrible'). The Prime Minister's demeanour shows he has taken ownership of the narrative and is probably lying but I can't prove it.

I tell my audiologist about the implants the CIA inserted in my brain during the last coma. He diagnoses paranoia and writes me a prescription for a handgun. I can't shoot the affliction left-handed so I'll just blast away at the leaf-blower.

Bec Kavanagh

STILL BOWIE

I loved you as the first notes of what might have been Bowie might have been Vanilla Ice played from the speakers in the tape deck of my poo-brown Beatle. *The woppy*, Dad called it. Metal built to withstand the war and the learner drivers of South Australia. It was Bowie. Of course.

I thought of you the day he died. Bowie. I was under pressure of my own. Mid-life. Divorce. Turkey puckered post birth skin.

Opening my eyes and realising I'd swum to the opposite corner of the pool again. Where am I? The chlorine burns my eyes, blurs the landmarks.

Alcohol blurs my anxieties, the stretch of time where the only fingers that reached for me were small, damp and covered in chewed up carrot.

Alcohol, motherhood, time blur the feeling of you on my lips. But it lingers enough to pinch together the edges of now to then.

The battery on my phone creeps down to a half-bar, then the yellow quarter, the red sliver. It will die soon. Almost time to say goodbye. Almost. One stupid earphone half-falling from my ear. The ones you like. Bowie still. Almost gone.

Jen Craig

JAMMING

Since it started less than a block into the walk, I got to thinking about that time I told you that the reason I hated putting on music, and particularly songs, was because it got inside of me – and not in a good way, I had tried to say.

Because I'd needed to make you understand that all it took for this to happen to me was that sometime after I'd heard the song, which is to say anything from hours to days – and it was usually worst with the shittiest song – *I want you baaaaaye-beeeee* – just the chance rhythm and speed of my steps as I walked along would be enough to slot one gear into another – mine into its – and there would be nothing I could do to prevent my self from being cranked along in its teeth.

Except that now, since I've been trying to work out the gears idea, I've been writing this down on my phone as I walk – not even caring that I look like someone who's addicted to her phone – and I have only just noticed that the wheel's gone quiet, and that maybe it was the writing that jammed it.

Jude Bridge

BARRAGE

Rain sounds like sausages frying in a pan. You don't think it does, right now, but after you've read this, it will rain, and it will forever after sound like sausages.

Eating too many sausages results in their rapid expulsion. Vomiting causes a chain reaction unmatched by any other physical body expression, excluding, arguably, the yawn.

Yawning leads to snoring, which angrily rammed-in earplugs do not drown out.

Drowning is supposed to be very peaceful, but I haven't tried it.

Peaceful isn't an option if you have tinnitus. There is no cure for tinnitus, or a neighbour who endlessly mows the lawn, whipper-snips, and chainsaws rogue hedges when not angle-grinding bricks. A nasty letter in his letterbox and spelling out the word 'wanker' with weedkiller on his manicured lawn has little effect.

Effective remedies for newborns do not exist. The joy of a new baby does not equal the sum of its crying parts. Best turn up Netflix.

Movie food is too loud. Next time you go to the real cinema, instead of cracking away at Maltesers, popcorn and crunchy potato chips, why not take hummus, bread rolls and peaches?

Endings are over-rated, so...

Liz Challoner

CALLING ELLIE

'Ellie, Ellie, Ellie.' He calls her name for eight hours without respite. The helpline states it's a chant. 'Offer a drink of water or a smoke.' The doctor declares it a brain loop. 'Ignore him and leave the room.' The repetition of her name takes her to a place she doesn't want to go. Water splashes his face. Two pairs of eyes stare; shocked, she even more than him. Silence. It starts again. 'Ellie, Ellie, Ellie.'

'Ellie, Ellie, Ellie.' Deep and loud. She tucks him into bed, tight, so he won't fall out. 'Try to sleep. I'll be back tomorrow.' His calling follows her down the dark timber stairs, only pausing as the back door closes.

The carers tell her he calls 'Ellie, Ellie, Ellie' all day. 'Is that you? Never says anything else.' He sits upright at the communal breakfast table. Quiet. Hair parted on the wrong side. Daintily eating a triangle of vegemite toast.

One sunny August day 'Ellie, Ellie, Ellie' stops. She'll never hear him say her name again. Then she remembers a security camera bought to watch him when she was out. It has video and audio playback. She presses his precious voice to her ear.

Kathryn Fry

WITH THE MOTHS ON ASH ISLAND

Harriet Scott has spent the day with the Emperor, her brush whispering precise colours to the page, every stage of its silent life down to each larval hair. The zigzag markings of outstretched wings, the plump flesh, the feathered antennae. She sets her brush on the bench and strides out into the whirr of wings about the mangroves by the Hunter River. As if the air hums in its own wind, an eddy here and there as moths fan close to her ear though none bruise her face. In the distance, water birds settle, the heat muffling their cries. So many quiet hours with the moths on Ash Island for this, her notable work. Her thoughts ring with impatience; she says it out loud and later writes it in her letter to Edward Ramsay, *Clearly I ought to have been Harry Scott instead of Hattie.*

Tim Heffernan

SKI TRAFFIC AFTER SUNSET

iceberg clouds nudge the range to my left while above my grand-mother's junket is the baked skin that holds an early moon in suspension. i am not driving so i learn the landscape. darkness robs the cloud of metaphor. now the flare run snakes from higher ground, winding down and around monaro spurs. in the dark i see white flung snow and in the silence of our opposite direction i hear the crisp cuts of skis on ice. we brake suddenly and are run off the road by some snow-blind ski car overtaking the stream, demanding the downhill right of way.

Christine Howe

SEA-WOMB

I was born in a shack next to the beach. Fibro, sepia-coloured. My parents used milk crates for chairs and washed their clothes in the shower. I have a photo of my very pregnant mother hosing down our ute on a patch of grass, Norfolk Island Pines in the background. You can't see the bright shock of the ochre-orange headland or the grey scrub rising behind the roof but they're there, solid, holding the sound of the ocean close in a bowl of craggy rock and sand.

Before my fingers knew the rough knobbles of melaleuca bark, before my eyes registered the limitless bright of the sky, I knew the sea of my mother's womb. The regular pulse of her blood. Her ebb and flow.

Today, I go to the clinic. There's a squelch of gel on the swelling bowl of my belly. I hear the regular pulse of my blood. The rhythm of it. Then the quickening flicker of another beat. The sweep of wind over spinifexed sand dunes, a clatter of crab claws on ochre-orange rock. And all of us – her, and she, and me – held in the womb of a thundering sea.

Elizabeth Tyson-Donely

STOVEPIPES

When you and I first met, we sat at the foot of the fire escape stairs, talking in the dark. I could smell the smoke that had soaked into your jeans. After saying something strange about *The Saints*, you ran your finger down the bare skin of my arm and quietly kissed my mouth. I dyed my hair black the next day.

We spent the week in my single bed, in a near empty apartment, watching TV, eating noodles and making each other laugh. You took your necklace off and gave it to me, the chain still warm from your body. As the record played, and the night closed in, we shed all memory of ever having been alone.

I'm in the bedroom getting dressed, when I hear you unlock the front door and drop your bag inside. You're breathing heavily from having walked up eight flights of stairs. It's always so hot on my birthday. I press my pendant to my lips and wait. I want you to play me a record.

Jennifer Kornberger

THE SNORER

she bought pink beeswax earplugs for Seb in Athens. *I won't hear the siren song tonight*, Seb joked. I am no longer beautiful to him, she concluded. her body noised without her permission, as if age was separating her into human and animal parts. *not that you aren't a musical nocturnal piglet*, he whispered, *the whole range from high wheezing to deep grunting.*

the next stop was Ubud, to get over the jetlag before hitting the Perth winter. to endure the tedious luxury of frangipanis placed on the bed, around their phones. she must be secretive, not speak about any sign of demise to avoid the extravagant precision of his naming.

she woke in the night to the sound of an animal pleading for its life. Kadek had told them earlier that a pig was to be slaughtered for tomorrow's ceremony. from the gully below came a frantic squealing followed by guttural groans. other pigs started up a melancholy and beautiful wailing. Sebastian muttered, *what is it?* she felt for his ears, pressed the beeswax more firmly into them. he must not hear this ravishing song. It was hers, this ungulate keening was for her ears alone.

Julie U'Ren

WHERE THERE IS NO FIRE

The silence was broken when the smoke alarm screeched at 1:50 am. It rang out urgently over and over. She stumbled out of bed, clattered about the room feeling for the light switch. In the kitchen, the broom fell out of the cupboard with a crack onto the floor. Fumbling with the handle – she prodded the air, cursing, unable to reach the small round button. The shrill ringing bounced on the walls and ceiling, filling the space, piercing her brain. She imagined emergency services arriving, finding her naked, wild-eyed and armed with the broom handle.

For months she'd been pushing notes through the gap under the neighbour's door. Repeated appeals to please – *turn the music down, quieten the barking dogs*. They'd never spoken. Clutching a robe around her nakedness, she crossed the hall and thumped heavily on his timber door.

Later when he folded the step-ladder, she thanked him. The screeching had stopped, but her head still throbbed with echoes of the alarm. It was 2:03 am. There was no fire and in the morning the dogs were quiet.

Richenda Rudman

WHEN IT WAS YUGOSLAVIA

When it was Yugoslavia, three young women and the hitchhiking lad they'd collected, stopped near a lake to photograph shots of sun that moved like fish on the water and mountains boasting alongside.

After, the van wouldn't start, and it was two days before they could fix it. They ate crusty bread and tomatoes, drank beer and sang around a campfire under the night's star-dense sky.

As the group was drifting off to sleep in the van, the engine of a truck rumbled closer and stopped, and a slide of the curtains revealed two soldiers, rifles over their shoulders. They slurred in their own language, drunk and staggering, calling for women. Inside the van, a fist was bitten, a face was white and a body reclaimed its foetal position.

When the soldiers banged their rifles on the roof, the hitch-hiker assumed the voice of a much bigger, older man and in the fragments of two languages, it was finally understood that his wives would remain sleeping.

Long after the country was dismembered by war, the three women spoke of the bravery of the young hitchhiker and the likelihood that the soldiers were dead.

Sigley Hood

ICE CUBE

I'm trapped in an ice cube. I'm the only cube in the icetray because nobody else in the house bothers to refill it.

It's breathtaking in here, an undisturbed beauty with perfect symmetry. It's a tight squeeze but I'm comfortable; I have my puffer jacket on, the hood pulled tight around my face, so only the tip of my nose is cold.

My family hovers over me. They're distorted, as if I'm looking through the lens of a heavy-walled soft drink bottle. I can't hear what they're saying but I can lip-read. *How did she get in there? Is she ok?*

Someone pops the icetray. I fall down to the bench and bounce onto the floor. I lock eyes with the dog. He knows it's me.

The family run around the kitchen, trying to devise a plan, but they keep bumping into each other. It reminds me of a scene from a slapstick movie.

The cube starts to melt and the noise of everyday life filters through – the dog barking, my husband yelling at the kids. I shout as loud as I can.

'Goddamn it, put me back in the freezer!'

But they can't hear me.

Ruth Wyer

RETURN POLICY

When Sound leased the two-bedder on Jackson Rd there was a party every weekend for two months. We'd always thought Graham had the best laugh amongst us, his head thrown back, his teeth swinging like old fence palings in the wind. Turns out he sounds like a Channel Billed Cuckoo and turns out not all birds have a song in their heart. Falling water, crunching gravel, turning pages – they were revelations but we hadn't known the tenuousness of sleep. Bottle-filled wheelie bins rattled down drives and we elbowed snoring partners and argued over the etiquette of late night flushing. Someone threw a Ratsak burger over the Miller's fence. It thankfully missed its target but it was the tipping point. We stood on her front lawn braying in protest at her closed blinds. But she was just as powerless; it continued to leach from her. She eventually left town without a word. Ironic, huh? We'd turned off the flash and vibration features on our alarm clocks. We woke late for work to find our neighbourhood returned to the smell of sprinklers and damp earth, and the sight of cockatoos bursting through Scribbly Gums – our hands dancing cautiously between us.

Mya Stewart

[READING SOUNDS]

[sound of voice being extracted]

[frustrated cries]

[frenetic silence]

[speaks in foreign language]

[clears throat]

[sighs]

[stammers]

[door opens, closes]

[sirens wailing in distance]

[heels scuffling on gravel]

[uncanny silence continues]

Angelica Hannan

ALL ROADS LEAD TO

The streets of Rome sound nicer in the dark: loud and wordless greetings; stilettos on the cobbled sidewalks; the simmering and spilling over of life for young and old.

On the hunt for gelati, we decide to *fare una passeggiata.*

Walking down Via del Lavatore, there starts a whisper, then a murmur, then a rumble in my ears, until I can't hear what we're talking about anymore. We turn a corner and suddenly the rumble is a roar that shouts out to me from the past. A roar that has been more than 270 years in the making. Before me, la Fontana di Trevi is a glimmering jewel in the inky night.

I wonder how many others have stood here in this very spot where I am now. Perhaps some other traveller, deafened by the water's noise, the chatter of so many others tossing coins with their right hand over their left shoulder, a hundred camera flashes exploding against the marble, has felt what I am feeling: the keys to the Eternal City are mine and mine and mine.

Biographies

JORDIE ALBISTON has published twelve poetry collections and a handbook on poetic form. Albiston possesses an ongoing preoccupation with mathematical constructs and constraints, and the possibilities offered in terms of poetic structure. Her work has won many awards, including the Mary Gilmore Award and the 2010 NSW Premier's Prize. She lives in Melbourne.

EMMA ASHMERE's short fiction has appeared in *The Age*, *Griffith Review*, *Sleepers Almanac*, and was shortlisted for the 2018 Overland/NUW Fair Australia Prize. Her novel *The Floating Garden* (Spinifex Press, 2015) was shortlisted for the 2016 MUBA.

DANIELLE BALDOCK's atmospheric writings capture small and vivid moments of time. She was published in Spineless Wonders *Landmarks* anthology in 2016, lives in Sydney and takes lots of photos. Her favourite colour is green.

KATHLEEN BLEAKLEY has three collections (with Ginninderra Press): *Azure*, 2017; *Lightseekers*, photography by 'pling, 2015; and *jumping out of cars*, with Andrea Gawthorne, images by 'pling, 2004. Kathleen's micro lit has been published in Spineless Wonders anthologies *Time* and *Writing to the Edge*.

JUDE BRIDGE is a two-hundred-year-old hobbit. She recently had a gig reading one of her surreal fictions at the Australian Short Story Festival. Her excitement levels peak when actors do justice to her stories at Little Fictions events.

JOHN CAREY is an ex-teacher of French and Latin and a sometime actor. The latest of his five poetry collections is *Duck Soup & Swansongs* (Ginninderra Press, 2018). Humour and satire figure largely in his work along with a quieter more lyrical mode.

BONNY CASSIDY is the author of three poetry collections, most recently, *Chatelaine* (Giramondo, 2017), which was shortlisted for the Prime Minister's Literary Awards and the Queensland Premier's Literary Awards. She lives in Naarm (Melbourne).

LIZ CHALLONER grew up in Melbourne and has lived in London. She has a lifelong interest in gaining access to narrow stairs and exploring where they lead. Her other interests include painting and photography.

JULIE CHEVALIER writes arty poetry and flashy fiction in Sydney. She is the author of three collections and co-editor of three anthologies. Her passion is helping asylum seekers find jobs.

SHADY COSGROVE is the author of *What the Ground Can't Hold* (Picador, 2013) and *She Played Elvis* (Allen and Unwin, 2009), which was shortlisted for the Australian Vogel Award. Her short fiction has appeared in *Best Australian Stories*, *Overland*, *Antipodes*, *Southerly* and other Spineless Wonder anthologies.

MOYA COSTELLO has two collections of short prose and two novellas. She's won arts grants and fellowships; has writing in journals, and anthologies (several from Spineless Wonders); and is adjunct lecturer, SASS, Southern Cross University.

JEN CRAIG's short stories have appeared in various Australian literary magazines. She has published a novel *Since the Accident* (2009) and a novella *Panthers and the Museum of Fire* (2015), which was longlisted for the 2016 Stella Prize. She has recently completed a creative PhD about transgenerational trauma and writing.

JAN DEAN has writing credits in *Not Very Quiet* (online), *Southerly*, *Meanjin*, *Rabbit Poetry Journal*, the *Weekend Australian* and *Newcastle Poetry Prize* anthologies. She was the first female president of Poetry at the Pub, Newcastle.

SHASTRA DEO was born in Fiji, raised in Melbourne, and lives in Brisbane. Her first book, *The Agonist* (UQP 2017), won the 2016 Arts Queensland Thomas Shapcott Poetry Prize and the 2018 ALS Gold Medal. Shastra's work has been published in *Meanjin*, *Ibis House*, and elsewhere.

LUKE EVANS is a high school teacher with a passion for writing. A father, librarian and careers advisor; a former poet, potato-picker, philosopher and a struggling smart-arse, Luke writes mostly for fun and release.

KATHRYN FRY has poems in various publications including the *Newcastle Poetry Prize* anthologies of 2014 and 2016. Her first collection, *Green Point Bearings*, was published by Ginninderra Press in 2018.

ALEXANDRA GENEVE is a West Australian writer and educator studying a Masters of Creative Practise at Curtin University. Her work has been published in *Elle Magazine*, the annual *Grieve Anthology* through the Hunter Writers Centre, and the literary journals *Meniscus* and *Pause*. She writes a blog at Medium.com.

ANGELICA HANNAN is a prize-winning flash fiction writer, daughter of a living saint, and the world's foremost authority on *Murder, She Wrote*. She lives in Sydney with her breathtakingly talented husband and their five heroic children.

TIM HEFFERNAN was awarded the 2016 joanne burns prize for his prose poem 'barunga conversations' and shortlisted in 2015 for 'butterflies in iraq'. He is co-editor of Verity La's, 'Clozapine Clinic – The Frater Project'.

HILARY HEWITT is a Sydney-based writer of poetry and fiction. Her work has been published in literary journals and anthologies. She was a runner-up in the 2013 joanne burns Award for microfiction and prose poetry.

RICHARD HOLT's micro-fiction collection, *What You Might Find* (Spineless Wonders, 2018) was described by *The Australian*'s Ed Wright as 'a tonic for readers in search of new angles from which to spin the world around in their heads'. When not writing he creates text-based installations and performances in public spaces.

SIGLEY HOOD is currently studying the Associate Degree in Professional Writing and Editing at RMIT. She reports that the story idea for 'Ice Cube' surfaced when she was sitting in a bar waiting to meet friends—her mind being obviously just loose enough.

CHRISTINE HOWE is a writer and academic who teaches at the University of Wollongong. Her poetry has appeared in *Cordite* and *Law, Text, Culture*, and her first novel, *Song in the Dark*, was published by Penguin.

JILL JONES has published eleven books of poetry, and a number of chapbooks. Recent books include *Viva the Real* (UQP), *Brink* (Five Islands) and *The Beautiful Anxiety* (Puncher & Wattmann), which won the 2015 Victorian Premier's Literary Award for Poetry. She is co-publisher, with Alison Flett, of Little Windows Press.

BEC KAVANAGH is a writer, reviewer and PhD candidate at LaTrobe University, where she explores the position of the female body in coming of age narratives. She is also the Stella Prize schools manager.

ANDY KISSANE writes fiction and poetry. Recent titles include the short story collection, *The Swarm*, and the poetry collection, *Radiance*, which was shortlisted for the Victorian and Western Australian Premier's Prizes and the Adelaide Festival Awards. andykissane.com

JENNIFER KORNBERGER is a writer and artist. She is currently working with poetic installation as contemporary ritual. theatreofthesea.net

BELLA LI is the author of *Argosy* (Vagabond Press, 2017), which won the 2018 Victorian Premier's Literary Award for Poetry and the 2018 NSW Premier's Literary Award for Poetry, and *Lost Lake* (Vagabond Press, 2018), which was shortlisted for the 2018 QLD Literary Award for Poetry.

DAVID MCCOOEY is a prize-winning poet. His latest book of poems is *Star Struck* (UWA Publishing, 2016). His poetry appeared in ten of the last eleven editions of *The Best Australian Poems* series. He is also a sound artist. His latest album (in collaboration with Paul Hetherington), *The Apartment*, was released in 2018.

SUSAN MCCREERY lives in Thirroul. She is the author of *Waiting for the Southerly* (Ginninderra, commended Anne Elder Award 2012), *Loopholes* (Spineless Wonders, finalist MUBA 2017), and *This Person Is Not That Person* (Puncher & Wattmann, forthcoming).

MARK O'FLYNN's novel, *The Last Days of Ava Langdon*, was a finalist in the 2017 Miles Franklin Award. It has also been short listed for the Prime Minister's Literary Award for fiction, and is winner of the Voss Award 2017. His latest collection of poems is the chapbook *Shared Breath* (Hope Street Press, 2017).

GEOFF PAGE is based in Canberra. He has published twenty-three collections of poetry, two novels and five verse novels Among his awards is the ACU Poetry Prize for 2017. His latest books include *Plevna: A Verse Biography of Sir Charles Ryan* (UWAP 2016), *Hard Horizons* (Pitt Street Poetry 2017) and *Elegy for Emily* (Puncher & Wattmann 2019).

A former English teacher, **BRENDA PROUDFOOT** lives on a farm in the Hunter Valley. Her short stories and creative non-fiction have been published by Catchfire Press, the *Newcastle Herald* and the Hunter Writers Centre.

SANDRA RENEW's current poetry project is the interrogation of LGBTIQAA gender discourses. Recently published *Who Sleeps at Night* (2017) and *The Orlando Files* (2018). Forthcoming *Acting Like a Girl* Recent Work Press (2019).

TESS RIDGWAY is currently completing a Masters of Research at Western Sydney University. She has been published in *Otolith*, the *Griffith Review*, *Axon Journal* and the *Meniscus Literary Journal*. Her work was performed at a Little Fictions night. She also facilitated a poetry group, Mutts.

MARK ROBERTS is a writer, critic and publisher based in the Blue Mountains west of Sydney. He is the founding editor of *Rochford Street Review* and his latest collection of poetry, *Concrete Flamingos*, was published in 2016

RICHENDA RUDMAN writes poetry and short stories and her work appears in numerous anthologies. In 2018, she has been a finalist in The Australian Catholic University's Poetry Prize and the Ada Cambridge Awards.

BRENDA SAUNDERS is a Wiradjuri artist and writer living in Sydney. Her third collection *Looking for Bullin Bullin* won the 2014 Scanlon Prize, the Woollahra Literary Prize and was short listed for the David Unaipon Award. Her work appears in many selected anthologies and poetry journals such as *Australian Poetry*, *Southerly*, *Overland* and *VerityLa*.

HAZEL SMITH was a Research Professor from 2007 to 2017 at Western Sydney University, where she is now an Adjunct Professor. She has published four volumes of poetry including *Word Migrants* (Giramondo, 2016), several academic books and numerous multimedia works. In 2018, with Will Luers and Roger Dean, she was awarded the Electronic Literature Organisation's Robert Coover prize.

PAULETTE SMYTHE lives in Melbourne where she teaches English to migrants and refugees. Her writing has previously been published in *Antipodean SF*, *Bewildering Stories*, *Verandah* and *Eureka Street*.

ANNA SPARGO-RYAN is the Melbourne-based author of *The Gulf* and *The Paper House*, and winner of the 2016 Horne Prize. Her work has appeared in *The Big Issue*, *Island*, *Kill Your Darlings*, *Meanjin*, *Good Weekend*, the *Guardian*, and many other places. She is a PhD candidate in Creative Writing at Deakin University.

BETH SPENCER's *The Age of Fibs* (now a Spineless Wonders ebook) won the 2018 Carmel Bird Digital Literary Award. Her other books include *Vagabondage* (UWAP, 2014) and *How to Conceive of a Girl* (Vintage, 1996). bethspencer.com

MYA STEWART is a first-year student in the Creative Writing program at RMIT University. Her work challenges 'hearing' audiences to think about how another body experiences sound. She experiments with poetic form as a way of grappling with the intersections of expression and memory.

CYNTHIA TROUP's creative work often emphasises the inherent musicality of language, and the allusive richness of fragments. Her texts have been performed in concert and theatre settings; her publications include essays, podcasts and poems. cynthiatroup.com

ELIZABETH TYSON-DONELEY is a writer of plays, poetry and memoir living in Brisbane. She has written and performed in the plays *The Magnificent Girl* and *The Seven Year Chaos*. Her poetry appears in several *Poetry d'Amour* anthologies and her micro-fiction is included in the Spineless Wonders anthology *Landmarks*. She has worked in both theatre and film production.

JULIE U'REN lives in Darwin. She is curious about the moments that change us and explores this in her flash fiction and short stories. Her writing has appeared in a number of anthologies and has been shortlisted for the Northern Territory Literary Awards.

KAREN WHITELAW is an award-winning Newcastle short story writer. Her work has been published in anthologies and literary journals in Australia and overseas.

RUTH WYER lives in southwest Sydney. Her stories have won a couple of competitions and have been published in several publications and anthologies. You can read more about that at ruthwyer.com or connect with her on twitter @ruthwyer.

Editor

CASSANDRA ATHERTON is an award-winning writer, academic and critic. She was a Harvard Visiting Scholar in English in 2016 and her most recent books of prose poetry are *Pika-Don* (Mountains Brown Press, 2017), *Prosody: Metre* (Recent Work Press, 2018) and *Pre-Raphaelite* (Garron Publishing, 2018).

She has judged many literary awards, including the Victorian Premier's Literary Awards: Prize for Poetry, The Lord Mayor's Prize for Poetry and the *Australian Book Review* Elizabeth Jolley short story competition.

The joanne burns Award

Each year Spineless Wonders auspices an award for the best writing in the forms of prose poem and microfiction in honour of foremost Australian experimental poet, joanne burns. The award is open to people residing in Australia and to Australians living overseas. Finalists chosen by each year's judging panel are offered publication in our annual anthology alongside invited writers.

The inaugural *joanne burns Award* was held in 2011 and was judged by joanne burns who selected Charles D'Anastasi's 'Madame Bovary' as the winning entry and commended Erin Gough's 'William Shatner vows to save the Great Basin Pocket Mouse' and Clare McHugh's 'Briefly'. All three pieces, along with those of other finalists appear in *small wonder*, edited by Linda Godfrey and Julie Chevalier.

The *2012 joanne burns Award* was judged by Carol Jenkins who selected Mark O'Flynn's 'under the maw of luna park' as the winning entry and commended Richard Holt's 'bush burial', Trina Denner's 'playing outside', Stu Hatton's 'down south' and Paul Mitchell's 'The Old Man and the Pool'. The winner and finalists all appear in *Stoned Crows & other Australian Icons*, edited by Julie Chevalier and Linda Godfrey.

The *2013 joanne burns Award* was judged by Shady Cosgrove who selected Mark Smith's '10.42 to Sydenham' as the winning entry and Hilary Hewitt's 'happy' and Mark Robert's 'cities that are not Dublin' as runners-up. All three pieces, along with those of other finalists appear in *Writing to the Edge*, edited by Linda Godfrey and Ali Jane Smith.

In *2014, The joanne burns Award* was judged by Angela Meyer and Richard Holt who selected Susan McCreery's 'Hold Up' as the winning entry and Kirsten Tranter's 'Turing Test Study Guide' and Mark Smith's 'The Meteorologist's Daughter' as runners up. All three pieces, along with those of other finalists are published in *Flashing the Square*, edited by Linda Godfrey and Bronwyn Mehan.

The 2015 joanne burns Award was judged by Kirsten Tranter who selected Nick Couldwell's 'Dancing' as the winning entry. Runners up were Tim Heffernan for 'Butterflies in Iraq' and Matthew Gabriel for 'jesussaves82'. All three pieces, along with those of other finalists and invited contributors are published in *Out of Place* edited by Kirsten Tranter and Linda Godfrey.

The 2016 joanne burns Microlit Award was co-sponsored by the Newcastle Writers Festival. The national category, judged by Cassandra Atherton, was won by Tim Heffernan for 'Barunga Conversation' and the Newcastle category, judged by Karen Whitelaw and Joanna Atherfold Finn, was won by Dael Allison for 'Breakwall'. The winning entries and finalists from both categories as well as invited contributors are published in *Landmarks* edited by Cassandra Atherton.

The 2017 joanne burns Microlit Award was co-sponsored by the Newcastle Writers Festival and judged by Cassandra Atherton. The national category was won by Tess Pearson for 'Traces' and the Hunter category was won by Luke Evans for 'You Can't Go Back'. The winning entries and finalists from both categories as well as invited contributors are published in *Time* edited by Cassandra Atherton.

About joanne burns

joanne burns grew up in Sydney's eastern suburbs. She worked as an English teacher in New South Wales, and for a time in London. She has taught creative writing in tertiary institutions, schools and community organisations. Her first collection of poems, *Snatch*, was published in London in 1972. Since then she has published more than a dozen further books of poetry. Her poems have appeared in numerous Australian literary journals, poetry magazines and have been set for study on the Higher School Certificate syllabus. joanne has been particularly concerned with the blurring of the distinctions between poetry and prose in her work, and has written extensively in prose poem/ microfiction forms. She has also written monologues and short futurist fictions and 'farables' (fables/ parables). Her latest collection *Brush* was published by Giramondo Poets in 2014. In 2016, she was awarded the New South Wales Premiers' Kenneth Slessor Literary Award for Poetry. A new collection of her work 'apparently' will be published by Giramondo Poetry in 2019.

Acknowledgements

We wish to express our appreciation to Deakin University for its support for this project.

Find more microlit at
SPINELESS WONDERS
www.shortaustralianstories.com.au

Spineless Wonders publications are available in print and digital format from participating bookshops and online. For further information, go to the Spineless Wonders website:

www.shortaustralianstories.com.au

www.ingramcontent.com/pod-product-compliance
Lightning Source LLC
Chambersburg PA
CBHW031028190726
48286CB00003BA/1065